I0557023

# The Third Wheel

## "Inside Out"

## Kristal Ben

ISBN:978-1-951838-08-9

Copyright © 2020 Kristal Ben
All rights reserved. Printed in the United
States of America. No part of this
publication may be reproduced, stored in a
retrieval system, or transmitted in any form
or by any means, electronic, mechanical,
photocopying, recording, or otherwise,
without the written permission of the
publisher.

Publisher: 90 Day Legacy Builders

# Table of Contents

# Preface

Feelings; everything written in the pages to come are just the feelings and life experiences of a young black woman. Life grants us all different paths and, most of the time, they all meet up somewhere because of certain similarities. When I came up with the title "The Third Wheel," I was at a place in my life where I was surrounded by people, yet so alone, distant, and different; well, in my mind at least. I can remember laying in the bed of my first apartment thinking I cannot be the only one who feels this way. Even though most life I have felt indifferent, I know invisible connections are all around. Consequently, and more literally than metaphorically, I was the actual "Third Wheel" on way too many occasions which in my mind made me the perfect candidate to speak on a subject as such for multiple reasons as you can see. As a fresh college graduate, my mind began to be fixated on a vision of a story: my story that I have held in for so long because of my uncomfortableness with vulnerability. BUT GOD, we are here now--the vision has manifested and I pray it blesses and inspires every eye and every person that comes into contact with it.

# Introduction

When using the term "the third wheel," many of our minds race to the unwanted person who tags along on a date; or the person who others feel pity for so they are allowed to accompany only due to compassion: the individual who tries their best to fit in places, knowing they really do not belong. To some, it may mean being the outcast: the outcast of a particular group, whether it be friends, family, sports team, class, or even a church. No matter the context, the term "the third wheel" does not have much positive association. Being the third wheel can cause one to become very uncomfortable with others around them as well as themselves. They may also begin to pretend to be someone they are not in order to fit into a specific group. Whether we want to admit it or not, as humans,

# Introduction

we all desire and require a sense of belonging; now, what we do, and where we decide to belong is partially on us. On the contrary, what do we do when we are placed in situations that are beyond our control? When the actions of others may not reflect what you are trying to be apart of or when you are surrounded yet still feel alone? You may possibly feel unworthy of your association with particular individuals because of your lack of connection to them. Like me, I am sure there are many who have felt this way at least once in their lifetime. I believe we all have desired to be apart of something that we were not qualified or ready for; however, we attempted this impossible feat anyway. There is someone who is racially unsatisfied and craves an understanding of why their skin is of a certain tone. Or someone that desires popularity but is outcasted because they look, think, or talk a certain way. Another attempts to follow the world's definition of physical beauty by reforming their physical attributes to make them more perceivable to the world. What do you do when you feel like God has dealt you the wrong hand of cards? When your desires and expectations for yourself become so clouded by your feelings of outcast that it shifts the focus from what you do have to what you do not have? Connection to a certain group has no direct link to individual purpose, especially if it is forced. Your purpose just may be in the opposite direction you are headed; a direction away from the assets or beliefs you are desperately trying to cling to. At some point, the focus must shift from being the third wheel to embracing the beautiful eccentricities that make you different. We all have a place where we belong--it is just up to us to find it and not force it.

# 1

## Questions

### "Why"

      To start, I wanted to tap into what I think is one of the most common and inevitable segments of life: questions. As a young child, we are taught how to ask and answer questions as a learning tool. We learn how to use it in a sentence with proper grammar so that it will make sense to those around us. Questions are for the most part easy to ask as we naturally have a desire to inquire about unknown things. It is how we grow, learn, and adapt to the environment around us. While asking questions may be easy, there are times where we face difficulty in finding the answers, which inevitably leads to more questions. Who do we ask? When do we ask? How do we even know what is the truth? With so much uncertainty surrounding questions, sometimes it is easier to not ask or think about it at all. What if it is not the answer we want or what if the answer never comes? Why are the necessary answers absent when we need them the most? These conundrums bring me to my next point and main objective of the real question, "Why"?

"Why:" one small yet oh so powerful word that just the slightest answer or clarification could change the very elements that shape you as a person. We want to know why, and I for one believe that we should know why, but, unfortunately, that is not how life works. Growing up as a young child, I had so many "why questions:" none that I or anybody else at the time seemed to have the answers to. I can remember specifically buying a book entitled *Why* and I just knew all of my answers I had been searching for would be smack dab in the middle of those few hundred pages; I was wrong. It did bring about perspective and gave me clarity in digging deep inside of myself to figure out the answer to my "whys." That, of course, is not what I wanted to hear or even think about. I wanted God to come down from his throne and meet me face-to-face and explain to me why; no soul-searching required: just straight-up answers. If we are all as intelligent as I believe, we all know that did not work out greatly in my favor. If only the answers to the puzzles of our lives are given to us that easily.

Personally, my struggle has always been feeling different and set apart. I did not understand it and, most of the time, if I am being honest, I hated it. I always thought that if I just knew why I was created the way I was, I could possibly come to terms with it easier. The unknown tortured my peace of mind. I wanted to know why I had to grow up where I did, why I was placed in the family I was in, why I looked a certain way, and why I lacked any real gifts or talents. Most of all, I was concerned with why God chose me; because, for as long as I can remember, I always knew he chose me, yet I just felt unworthy of being chosen. I never truly knew exactly what I was chosen for: I just always felt different. The questions kept coming and I wanted to know why I was shy and quiet growing up and why speaking in front of crowds made me nervous. I questioned why I had what is now considered "resting bitch face" which gives off the impression that I am consistently mad at the world. For clarification, I am not mad at the world or at anyone; it is truly just how I look and I have convinced myself it is totally out of my control.

I am actually the complete opposite and it takes a lot to make me thoroughly upset which is why I find it ironic that people make that assumption. In addition to my uncertainties, in my spare time, I always found time to inquire about why I was so introverted and that a day at home with a good book or music playing in my ears was far more appeasing to me than going out to the nearest bar or club. I could go on for an eternity with all of the "whys" I was stuck with in my head. Some are small in importance while others can literally keep me up all night awaiting solutions. I am pretty confident we all go through this and have our own personal list of questions we are waiting to yell at God when we finally meet him. Growing from a little girl to a twenty-six-year-old woman, I still have moments of confusion. What I have learned to do is live with my questions and embrace everything about me--even if it makes me feel oddly alone.

I am a firm believer that God knows what he is doing and the mysteries of life is what makes it so beautiful. I do not think we could truly imagine a life with no questions of "why." Like really, if we knew the answers to everything, we would have nothing to look forward to. Questions keep our minds fresh with opportunities to learn and grow as individuals. It forces us to challenge ourselves and others, and, most importantly, it keeps us going.

Self-reflection is the result of "why" questions. It forces us to tap into a certain part of our hearts and brains to get those difficult answers. Since I am introverted, my mind naturally navigates towards thinking and coping internally when seeking answers to questions or problems that may arrive. The bottom line is: when we specifically have these "why" questions, it is up to us to figure out the answers to them. Most of the time, it is internal dilemmas and not external predicaments that burden us, so the need to involve others is usually irrelevant. Often times, there is no tangible solution and even great advice that end with you needing to personally decide to make the change. I am specifically referring to those questions that cause you to be vulnerable. Not the questions you ask your friends or your parents: the ones where you are totally alone and cannot help but wonder: "why am I like this." It could be regarding physical attributes, personality traits, family placement, or monetary value. Once you realize what your "why" is, I want to challenge you to not ignore it. Often times, we run away from facing the difficult atrocities in life head-on because it forces us to be honest with ourselves. Here is a small secret: there is healing in honesty. Ignoring your "whys" will not make them go away. Therefore, the next time the "whys" creep up, confront them. You may not get all the answers (or any at all), but acknowledge them and work through getting the clarity you need. Whether that involves praying, meditating, or relaxing, commit to confronting and not running.

# 2

## UNO Out

"The Wrong Hand"

Imagine it is a Friday night, and all of your friends are off of work with you and you all decide to have a game night full of card games and drinks; just a night of good, old-fashioned competition. The first game you all decide to play is UNO since it seems to be both the most common, fun, and controversial game known to man since no one knows the actual rules. You are excited and ready to win so that your friends have nothing to hang over your head. As the game begins and the cards are being dealt, you notice the slight grin on your friends' faces from the satisfaction from the cards they have been dealt. As it gets to you, you are greeted with utter disappointment; each card handed to you only seems to make your hand worse. You immediately think how it is so unfair that you have to already start from behind merely because your hand was trash; however, you went on to finish the game and, of course, came out dead last as you blamed it on your terrible hand.

What do you do when you feel like life has given you the wrong hand of cards? Do you pout and complain? Do you already accept defeat since playing from behind is difficult in itself that it makes actually coming back to win seems nearly impossible? Lastly, do you attempt to do your best with what was given to you? Often times, I believe we sometimes feel that we were not given the right cards to properly live life effectively, living a defeated lifestyle because of it. We resent others who we believe got "a silver spoon" when in actuality they may have gotten "a brown spoon." There are so many different sayings like "everything that glitters isn't gold" or "the grass isn't greener on the other side" and they are all true. No one has the perfect life--we have all been given a few bad cards no matter how it may look to the outside world. Yet, how we choose to play our cards is all unique. It is for this reason that two people can come from the same, successful household, yet one can become an addict of drugs while the other makes it to be a big-time lawyer. Learning to become triumphant in adversity is key.

Unfortunately, we are unable to choose everything in our lives like our families, genetic makeup, physical appearances, or personality traits. I for one choose to believe that it does us more good than harm actually. The problem is not being born into the wrong family or not looking a certain way or having certain monetary means. The problem is developing insecurities or lack of initiative and drive for yourself because of those circumstances you wish you could change. To be fair, some individuals have had a difficult life since birth and I can only imagine the mental toil it has had on them. But God can take the worst of the worst and change it into the best of the best. Jeremiah 1:5 states that "Before I formed you in the womb I knew you, before you were born I set you apart." Then, in Jeremiah 29:11, "For I know the plans I have for you, declares the Lord, plans to prosper you and not to harm you, plans to give you hope and a future." This just so happens to be one of my favorite scriptures that keeps me encouraged that I will speak more about later on. If God purposely dealt you the hands of your life and still has a plan for you, who are we to be weary and doubt our greatness just because we have to start a little from behind; some further than others? Where you come from does not determine where you end up.

I've been there. I've been that person who has complained and felt like I was always playing from behind. I never understood why God made me a certain way, or why I went through certain hardships. Everything felt wrong and I knew He made a mistake because there was no way He desired for me to be that miserable. I asked for a way out, I asked for the impossible: for life to change that I knew could not be changed, but, at the time, I felt like it needed to. I had to learn that those very few alterations that I wished were never apart of my story were the very things that would make my story unique. I challenged myself to shift focus from frowning upon certain elements in my life to slowly loving them. Knowing the lessons I know now, I look back at previous moments in my life that were clouded by dissatisfaction. I realize I spent far too many years resenting the most beautiful magnanimities about me. We lack nothing and we have everything we need; but somehow complaints manifest themselves daily because of our surroundings. The first step to shifting my focus was killing the monster of comparison.

I like to think of comparison as a silent enemy, and today with social media, it is difficult not to engage in its foolishness. Here is my reason on why comparison is so dangerous. Comparison only results in one of two detriments: either self-entitlement and arrogance or despondency and self-pity. When you compare yourself to others, you either feel like you are doing exceptionally better than others or like you're not doing enough and beneath others--both of which can be harmful to someone's true identity. Comparisons bring dissatisfaction and a lack of trust in

God's timing simply because you see it happening to others around you. Even feeling superior to those around you can lead to a false sense of self and cause contentment in areas of life that are destined for growth. It is these comparisons that feed the notion of being dealt the wrong cards and not maintaining a certain level of success for reasons that are beyond your own fault. It is emotionally draining to constantly feel like you are starting from behind. To constantly compare yourself to where others are in relation to you is throwing gasoline on a burning flame. It only magnifies the turmoil that is already there.

The impulse to want to control everything around you can be normal but can create inferior feelings when you are not in control. Everything happens for a reason and you are who you are for a reason. Your family, awkward tendencies, and strong attitude are just pieces of the puzzle that help complete you. You are forever in control of your own destiny; and, even though what you have and where you come from differs from society, you may still have anything your heart desires. If you are still convinced that you were born with a bad hand; remember, a good comeback or underdog stealing the game from behind makes a far better story than the expected happening. Execution is key.

# 3

## Outcast(ED)

I'm going to go out on a limb here and say that I am not the only one who has been the third wheel before. Whether it be in the form of two people with you on a date or merely tagging alongside your siblings and some friends, no matter the actual situation, I am pretty sure it was not the ideal occasion. Being that one person who cannot engage in certain conversations, you stare at your phone and pretend to not be listening to the things around you-- this can be awkward and annoying. Since I am overly dramatic, I have come to the conclusion that I have been in that situation way more than the normal individual. I have easily surpassed the limit beyond what is acceptable. Additionally, over time, I grew accustomed to being invisible yet present because I always felt outcasted. Contrary to what some may believe, I did not fit in most places I found myself. I always seemed to stick out like a sore thumb. However, there are levels to this because there are times that I do fit right in. To some, I could be considered popular, but I like to think of myself as a popular loner because I feel most content when I am alone and not around others. When it comes down to who I truly am and how I think, *uncommon* is the best way to describe it. Feeling outcasted has been what I considered both a blessing and a curse on my life. I never truly wanted to be like everyone else so being different made me happy; but, I also wanted to feel accepted and able to relate to others. I spent most of my life learning how to manage the two and how to make them both work out for me in a way that was satisfying for me.

Growing up shy, I always felt invisible being that I could make my presence barely noticeable. I hated being so shy, but I hated attention even more. I can remember doing obnoxious actions to be liked by people that I later realized I had nothing in common with. I would give money or say yes to any and everything simply to belong. Deep down inside, I knew it did not feel natural, but I wanted to feel normal: I needed to feel normal. Thankfully, as life goes on and personal development and growth takes place, I can say I have done both. I have witnessed what it feels like to be part of the crowd while I have also been exposed to being outside of the crowd. I went through stages of growth that caused me to test out the waters of everything I wanted to experience. One truth that cannot be forgotten is that you cannot run from you. Who you are will follow you for the rest of your life. In those late nights when there is no one else around, the real you is more clear to see and understand. As humans, I think we subconsciously want to hide our true identities because we fear rejection; we become surface people. We show the attributes we want you to see and hide the very gifts that make us unique. Our insecurities automatically choose for us what others will and will not accept. As a defense mechanism to protect ourselves, we are always on guard. Therefore, we put on a smile and show all the qualities that seem acceptable to the outside world and inside we still feel alone. It is for this reason that most people only know of me, but do not know me.

The word *outcasted* carries a negative connotation since it means to be kicked out of something as if it never deserved to be there. I choose to look at it in another light of simply

meaning "set apart." What makes us
so beautiful is that we are all
uniquely made and no two people
are exactly alike. We have all been
set apart: each person just chooses
to embrace themselves in different
ways. Some attempt to escape from
what makes them set apart in ways
that I did as a child and others
welcome it and pride themselves on
it. No matter where you are in your
life, if you feel "different" or
"outcasted," I challenge you to
embrace it. Now I can admit that
saying that you are going to embrace
it is not as easy as actually doing it.
Actions are far harder to follow
through than pointless words. Doubt,
fear, and uneasiness will present
themselves in the beginning
moments and try to make you feel
like something is wrong with you. I
cannot even begin to remember how
many times I asked God, "Why did
you make me this way?" I wondered
why I had no desire to do what
others around me were doing. I

wanted to know why my thought
process was different and why I
always seemed to care about facets
that mattered to no one but me. At
some point, it hit me, and I realized I
looked differently, I analyzed things
differently, I loved differently, and I
spoke differently. While some may
say viewing yourself as different and
unique comes off as arrogance, I am
reminded that if I had it my way, I
would have never chosen to be
this way. As I stated before, there
are levels to this and the dreadful
feeling of no one ever understanding
you because you are you, and the
only one like you, is a feeling I would
not wish upon my worst enemy.
Constantly feelings left out or
uninterested in the world can be
shameful for the person living that
reality. Furthermore, to feel like the
pedestal before you has been placed
so high that if you somehow fall shy
of living up to the expectations your
whole life will crumble is vexing. If
you are like me, at some point you

get tired and you give in. You do all the goals you have always wanted to do, and you make yourself feel happy. You do not let any rules or perceptions you have of yourself hinder you from living in the moment. For once, you decide to not be an outcast: you decide to be in, and being in feels good.

Remember earlier when I said that you cannot run from you; you can try, but God is humorous enough to bring you right back to where you belong. The very quirk that you despise can be the one specialty another is praying for. The qualities you frown upon in yourself can be exactly what others love about you. Being confident in knowing that you are set apart and living it out will attract others who are similar to you or even encourage someone to live in their truth. God will place people around you that needs to be around you. How tragic it is for us to hide the pieces of us that the world needs to see simply for a false surface version of ourselves. We all have unique qualities; therefore, we should be unapologetically us. I once saw a quote that exposed: "I'd rather be an outcast now than be cast out later."

# 4

# Me, Myself and I
"LonelIness"

"We are all born alone and die alone. The loneliness is definitely part of the journey of life."--Jenova Chen

One of the motivations that fed the notion of me feeling different or weird is my obsession and complete satisfaction with being alone. The introverted side of me finds joy in having days where I do not engage with anyone; and, to be completely honest, sometimes I would rather it always be that way. Some would argue and say it is a bad habit of an unhealthy lifestyle being that we need relationships and people to function normally. While I agree with that statement, I still unapologetically feel most at peace when it is just me. I love other people, my friends, family members, co-workers, and other associates I come across daily, but my distant tendencies seem to come naturally to me. The struggle that takes place is when what comes naturally to you is almost the complete opposite of what the rest of the world deems normal which can cause feelings of estrangement.

Introverts! I can remember being young and afraid to admit that I was an introvert, even though everything about me screamed it so effortlessly. I felt ashamed of the fact that I could care less to go out and socialize and nearly despised talking in front of crowds. I would much rather be reading in my bed with a book in my hand, binge-watching a new television show, or blasting music to my ears. I hated small talk and found far more interest in deep conversations ranging from religious preferences to conspiracy theories and anything that stretched the mind to think beyond normal life activities. I have always kept a small number of friends and never had a desire to have many since my lack of trust and opening up to others have always been a weakness of mine. From my perspective, the world portrayed being an introvert as being weak and submissive since aggression is not typically one of our strong suits. We internalize everything which can sometimes lead to impulsive desires to be in control which can cause overthinking. We typically ponder and consider every possible outcome before acting on a decision. Even as an adult through job hunting, I always felt like the system was set against us introverts. I never knew how to truly answer those questions that asked "do you enjoy being alone?, do you consider yourself quiet?, are you the first to hop at doing a task?" If you can relate to feeling uneasy during that interrogation, then maybe you also felt uncomfortable about answering these questions honestly out of fear of not getting a job because you would rather work alone than in a group--all along, knowing that just because you are quiet or introverted does not mean that you are unable to adapt or adjust to an extroverted world; we still have to survive. It could be just me, but I always felt like being completely honest would do me more harm than good. I would verbally deny certain accusations in order to fit in and make people believe I could be apart of the crowd and enjoy being the center of attention while knowing deep down inside just the thought of having all eyes on me makes me cringe to this day. I thought that if I convinced them with my words, then maybe my actions would naturally follow suit. This is when the battle of trying to be someone you are not starts to get the best of you. Believe it or not, I would always rather be home; granted, I do not let this stop me from going out and enjoying myself. However, best believe returning to my place of comfort is always a major highlight of the night. With that being said, growth is still necessary and comfort zones yield progression. So it is vital that you do all the actions that make you scared and nervous and push you beyond your limits. That is how you slowly turn your weaknesses into strengths. Over time, I learned to understand the balance between who I am and who I am trying to become.

Some people hate the thought of being alone, and then there is me. There is nothing frightening or uneasy about it to me: I welcome it and look forward to it. My comfortability with being by myself is one of the main reasons I have always felt outcasted and like a typical third wheel for most parts of my life. I also would not normally verbally offer up that information to others which played a role in me believing I was so rare. Now that I am older, I realize there are far more people out there who enjoy being alone like me that I seemed to be unaware of before. I can remember growing up as a "Preacher's Kid" and everyone had their assumptions of how your life was and how strict your parents were. Surprisingly to most, my parents were never overly strict in a way that we were held captive to the world. I personally chose to stay home most of the time and refused invites because I valued being alone and, at times, struggled with entertaining others. I was not forced--I preferred being a loner. If I somehow found myself constantly surrounded by other loners, life would be semi-perfect. I have always navigated toward being alone easily for the simple fact that most of my life I have been alone; or, for better lack thereof, felt alone. Constantly feeling distant or like you do not belong everywhere you go forces you to want to be alone; with yourself, you never have to pretend. I was never a stranger to myself. I was very much in tune with my thoughts and everything else I uniquely consisted of. Unfortunately, due to lack of acceptance, my insecurities forced me to keep most of those features to myself and to never want to put them out on display for anyone other than myself to see or know.

I would like to believe there is a distinct difference between being "alone" and "lonely." In my definition, alone literally means having no one around whereas lonely is a feeling that stems from feeling completely separated from others. It is possible for a person to be completely alone without being lonely. Loneliness can stem from a level of seclusion from a group of people or the world in general while yearning to feel included, but failing to succeed in doing so. It could be mentally challenging and draining especially since someone can also be completely surrounded by individuals and still feel lonely on the inside. It is for those reasons that one can be satisfied with being alone and actually prefer it; however, feeling lonely is normally one of those feelings we attempt to avoid and shake its existence if presented in our lives. Personally, loneliness is a very rare feeling for me because I hardly yearn for the company of others. I am usually content with just being alone most of the time. I am human, and, consequently, I do have moments where I feel overwhelmingly lonely. The negative feelings associated with loneliness usually do not last long for me as I quickly recover because of my familiarity with being alone. Be cautious to not confuse the two; being alone can be healthy, but too much alone time can lead to possible loneliness as well. Too much of anything can cause more harm than good. Loneliness, which is similar to feeling deserted and abandoned, can possibly lead to more depressing feelings and possible mental breakdowns.

The idiosyncrasies I despised in myself when I was younger were the very characteristics I learned to praise myself for and deem beautiful as a young adult. There is a special gift in learning how to be alone; not a total state of contentment with it, but it is necessary. When the distractions in your life start to become more influential and important than self-sustainment is when the focus has become lost. You cannot be so focused on the foibles around you that you forget to take care of you. Mental days are significant, and days spent alone are equally as important. It is not imperative to always answer the phone and offer a listening ear. You do not have to constantly say "yes," and sometimes a simple "no" could save your life, both literally and figuratively. Balance is the key to self-sufficiency, and too much or too little of anything will throw you off. Time alone is essential and can promote self-growth by giving us time to reflect, plan, and execute what we actually want for ourselves. Moreover, time with loved ones helps satisfy those feelings of belonging that we all need no matter how much we may try to deny it. They both serve their own special purpose. If you often find yourself making yourself busy to avoid being alone at all costs, maybe it's time to consider figuring out why. Do you truly like yourself; or are you possibly running from the inevitable of making tough decisions and subconsciously diverting your attention elsewhere? We are all uniquely made and handle adversities in ways that are best for us, but turning your weaknesses into strengths is the only way to become the best version of you. As stated previously, find your weakness, and make it a strength. God does his best work through us when He has our undivided attention.

# 5

## Sense of Belonging
### "Me Too"

As humans, we all have a natural desire of wanting to belong. God specifically made us in ways where we naturally belong. Whether it be by gender, race, family affiliations, sexual orientation, or astrology. In some way or another, we belong to a certain group of people. This desire to fit in is human nature and can hardly be controlled because man was not made to be alone. Problems can, however, arise when we start to attempt to belong where we are not intended to belong or when we are unsatisfied with the groups that we do naturally belong to. Some may feel stuck in believing that the subjective place they have been predestined to belong to is indeed a place that they arguably do not belong.

We have all been placed in situations that are beyond our control and, at times, our minds cannot seem to fathom why circumstances are the way they are. The need to feel of importance to someone or something remains in our subconscious mind waiting for an opportunity to terrorize us when presented with opposition. There are times where we may attempt to convince ourselves that belonging is unnecessary and that we are better off alone. Unfortunately, for those who fight the need to belong, that battle is typically lost because we are purposely wired to fit somewhere. At some point, we must come to the realization that we need people, groups, and connections within the two. There is no fault in desiring to belong to a certain group; I honestly consider that a healthy way of thinking. Some may find it difficult to adapt to and find acceptance in the groups that we feel we were unfairly placed in. This battle that starts in the mind can create mental frustration if not handled wisely.

I can remember being a young girl having doubts and lacking acceptance in having a sense of belonging. In contrast to the demeanors I possessed on the outside, I felt very few emotional and spiritual connections. During my youth, my most significant struggle was not believing that I fit in with my family. The gifts I seemed to be good at differed from those around me and my impulsive obsession with comparisons only left room for negative thoughts to creep in. I never paid much attention to what I did have; my focus was primarily on what I did not possess. Family can be such a sore spot for many people because we have no input concerning its biological attachments; and, although so many of us wish we could be in control, I believe God purposely designed it that way for a reason. I was so focused on not having the right pieces of the puzzle to fit where I supposedly belonged that I convinced myself that God made a mistake. Ignorantly at the time, I forgot that puzzle pieces can be tricky. Sometimes a piece may look like it initially does not fit so we move on and try another one. Other times we try to force a piece to fit in its undesignated place and get upset at the result of an incomplete puzzle. Most of the time we are impatient; therefore, we convince ourselves we have it wrong while our anger and uncertainty blind us, making us unable to see that we have had all the right pieces all along. At some point, if we keep at it and allow ourselves to understand that God makes no mistakes, we realize we were right where we belonged to the whole time.

As I mentioned, "The grass is not greener on the other side" is one of the most common aphorisms used to teach us to appreciate what we have instead of yearning for what others have. I remember growing up and watching the television show entitled *Full House*. I remember being fascinated with the family and wanting to raise a family of my own one day just like them. I paid attention to the features that appealed to me and my emotions. I was fixated on the items they possessed that I felt I lacked, but not once did I consider the valuable possessions that I occupied that they did not. This is what I mean about perception; the mind is vastly complex and, if pessimism is what you naturally gravitate to, it will become all you see. Now that I am older, I take a different approach in realizing the blessings I had that they did not. In the show, the girls did not have a mom: she passed away. It never dawned on me to even consider that dynamic playing a role in how their lives were further constructed. I only saw the disadvantages that benefited my feelings of discontentment. I saw green grass, but I was mentally unable to see the unhealthy patches or the rain that helped produce what I imagined to be good. I was spared of the opportunity to see the hardships that played a pivotal role in their journey, yet I did not initially see it that way. It is in these lessons and moments that I realized that my race, gender, family dynamics, physical attributes, and every other nuance that I consisted of was no mistake.

As you grow and evolve as a person, you look back at your life and wish you could have a do over. The missed opportunities could haunt you in your present life. I can confidently say we have all mumbled the words "if I knew then what I know now" at least once. I spent countless amounts of time trying to fit into places and with people that I was never intended to fit into that I lacked clear visibility of the blessings I was already apart of. Since our desire to belong is a part of our natural biological make-up, it is essential that we learn to not only live with but love and accept the features that we cannot change. We were all born into certain groups and categories of people without consultation. I find it highly unlikely that there is a person alive who has total adoration for every aspect of their life. There are some conditions that we can control like our friends, schools, or careers; we personally choose to belong there. When those areas no longer satisfy us or bring us the happiness we desire from them, we can easily blame ourselves and thankfully have the opportunity to change it. Sadly, not everything in life can be changed with just the snap of a finger. Some circumstances, no matter how far you try to run away from, will always follow you because it makes you who are. It is up to us to begin to embrace the essences  that we despise that cannot be changed rather than bear the burden of living life unsatisfied. Change your mindset; change your life.

We all belong to something. No matter how lonely or different we may feel, we all fit somewhere. Believe it or not, there is a spot where your puzzle piece belongs. It would be foolish of any of us to believe that acceptance of this is easy, especially when we feel unworthy of belonging or would rather belong elsewhere. Both of which are normal feelings; however, I attempt to challenge myself and others to find the silver lining. Yes, you were created different, as each of us were and, at times, you may seek to understand why you do not identify with certain groups of people. How boring would this Earth be if everyone appealed to the same individualities  or physically looked the same way? We were all born of a mother and, even in our differences, we could never truly be alone. Often times, the fight in our minds are far more challenging than the forces pulling at us in the flesh, and our thoughts inadvertently make us feel outcasted. Even with all the uncertainty and lack of understanding of the word "why," we must believe that we were specifically designed for a reason and embrace our uniqueness. At some point, the focus must shift from asking "why" and navigate toward asking "what". A simple question to begin with is: "Knowing who I am and loving all of my differences, what is it that life requires of me? How can my differences be utilized to promote purpose for my life and those around me?" Once we begin to welcome who we are, where we belong, and why we were placed there, life will all start to make sense. You will no longer feel the need to project yourself elsewhere or loathe in the feelings of defeat. You will finally grasp the concept of "me too" while embracing the different qualities that makes you *you.*

# 6

## I Love Me, NOT!

I remember watching a Tyler Perry movie and there was a part in the movie in which a couple was struggling in their marriage. The woman was advised by her friend to make a list and divide it into the good endowments she loved about her husband and marriage and a list stating the bad. She was told that if the bad outweighs the good, to let it go, but if the good outweighs the bad, to fight for her marriage. As I watched this scene while dealing with my own personal self-esteem issues, I decided to utilize that same concept to internalize my personal demons. I can remember compiling a list and on one page it said, "Things I love about myself" and on another side it said "Things I hate about myself". Human people have human feelings and, contrary to what most would believe because of what I decide to show to the outside world, the things I hated about myself were highly numbered in comparison to the things I loved. Therefore, I was at a crossroads asking what does it imply if the bad outweighs the good in my situation? I was helpless and felt like there was nothing left to fight for. I spent most of my time wallowing in self- pity and feeling sorry for myself. I knew in that fight I was all alone because no one would understand the seriousness behind it or even believe me. Realistically, I knew there was no one for me to turn to about these feelings; how could anyone truly understand the depths of what I was feeling and help offer me a way out? I concluded that venting was not necessary or beneficial for me as no one could teach me how to love myself but God and myself.

Battles fought in the mind are battles meant to destroy you mentally. Your mind has to be protected at all costs because, once the mind is tampered with, the physical body normally follows. I find it so much easier to deal with problems when they involve other people. In today's society, you may effortlessly block, unfriend, and physically stay away from those who cause you harm. You may choose to either ignore the negativity or you may confront it. Normally in that confrontation, a solution is found and typically sets the standard for handling similar situations that may arise. Imagine the issue not being with other people. Imagine the issue not being your job, lack of money, sickness, or anything else tangible. Imagine the problem literally being *you*. The internal battle that you are fighting takes place in your mind and your thoughts cause you to hate and lack satisfaction with what you have. Internal dilemmas can cause external stagnation because it is mentally draining and difficult to handle "you" problems. When confronting these mental roadblocks, you are forced to deal with the things you have either been running from or pushed to the back of your mind. There will come a time where you may come to realize that your biggest enemy is yourself. You begin to come to terms to see that everything that you are going against is only forces in your own mind. Once you can get past the enemy in yourself, you will become unstoppable.

True intimacy and honesty with oneself is a major key in succeeding in self-sufficiency and confidence. Learning and being honest with yourself about your strengths and weaknesses is what will promote self-growth. Often times, we lack acknowledging the unpleasantries thinking they will just go away over time. Personally, I had to allow all the detestation I had for myself to play out. I had to dig deep into the qualities that I despised about myself and figure out the root of the hate. Most of it all stemmed from my feelings of outcast and feeling indifferent and uneasiness of never feeling apart. However, as previously mentioned, the silent killer that stole my joy for a brief period in my life was, of course, the art of comparison.

Being as optimistic as I can be, I would bet my last belief that no one truly hates themselves. Sometimes it is as simple as your dissatisfaction with your insufficiencies having more influence on you than your satisfaction of your sufficiencies. We live in a society where we see everything. We see the good, the bad, and the ugly. We see the atrocities we hope to never experience and we see all of our dreams lived vicariously through

other people. We see the world's perception of
physical perfection which changes so effortlessly, yet we try to keep up with its timeless trends. The need to constantly keep up with a world that thrives off of change and economical differences is a path often taken without notice. Many times, we are ignorant to the fact that we are comparing ourselves and creating false images of ourselves with ideas that was never meant to be a part of our destiny. Sometimes, we lack knowledge and understanding of the depth of our desires to be like others which inadvertently causes dislike for ourselves. So no, I do not believe that we hate or despise ourselves; I just think we want to be like "that" whatever that is. We may want to attend *that* school, get married at *that* age, be *that* size, have *that* amount of money, have *those* designer clothes, or have *that* family. We can become so focused on desiring and paying more attention

to the wants we do not have and forget the beauty in what we do have and who we are. There are parts of you that someone else would love to possess; we are just too busy looking elsewhere to even recognize it. The very thing you despise could be the dream of someone else.

Perception is everything and how you decide to view life is up to you. You can give two different people the same problem and they will go about solving it in two separate ways. There is optimism and pessimism and I have had my share of experiences with both. I know what it feels like to see victory in the midst of turmoil and I know what it feels like to believe the world is falling apart at all times. Proverbs 23:7 states: "For as he thinketh in his heart, so is he." One of my biggest roadblocks has always been thinking the worst and, consequently, believing the worst. Outside of my belief in God, if I didn't see it, it was hard for me to believe because I lacked faith. My lack of faith allowed me to miss out on many opportunities that I felt unworthy of. When you know better, you do better. I have constantly heard people say speak into the atmosphere and I never truly understood speaking something that I never truly believed; I had it backwards. I wanted to believe it and then speak it when the key is to speak it until you believe it and believe it until you see it.

Learning to love yourself unapologetically brings a certain level of peace that we all deserve to experience. I mean truly loving yourself, not just stating that you do for outside validation. In actuality, speaking it into existence is a powerful tool that can be utilized for personal belief as well. Those piercing thoughts when no one else is around are the ones that matter; you cannot run or hide from them. They either build your character up or tear it down. To love all the attributes about yourself that makes you different allows you power, especially when you learn to love what you once hated. Embrace every insecurity just like you would every strength. From every piece of hair on your head to the lisp that may come out of your mouth when you speak. Believe it or not, somebody needs you just the way you are.

# 7

# Complete

"Restoration"

It could be assumed that it is universally known that the number seven means completion. Whether you look at the word *complete* as an end to a beginning or in the context of meaning whole, both are fit for this occasion. Within the previous pages, I spoke about loneliness, helplessness and thoughts of abandonment and feelings of outcast. Even with those variations of feelings, there is still a place of restoration and completeness to be achieved. Let's say you have identified yourself with feeling some of the things previously stated but you find yourself still in self-doubt and struggling with full acceptance of yourself. If I am allowed, I would like to offer spiritual guidance on what I pondered on to allow myself to get to the place that I am today.

I believe that one of the first steps to healing is admitting to yourself that something was broken in the first place. A wound cannot be healed if you continue walking around like it is non-existent-- ignoring it only tends to make it worse. Acknowledge the pain, then take the steps necessary to heal. Often times, we skip the acknowledgment and continue walking around with open wounds and wonder why time after time we still feel broken. It is okay to not be okay; however, being able to admit those feelings is the only way to conquer them. At some point, we have to gain control of the negative thoughts that try to destroy us. Sometimes even with all the love and adoration we carry for ourselves, we still have our moments of uncertainty which is normal; yet, we cannot allow ourselves to become fixated on those thoughts. This all leads us to the golden question of how do we learn to live and love the parts of ourselves that the world neglects or shames. Disclaimer!: I do not have all the answers nor am I an expert in the subject, but I have had life experiences that have taught me to go through and grow through everything that came my way. Even with my feelings of lacking purpose and loneliness, I was able to take control of my thoughts and teach myself how to love every inch of myself while managing being different. Once you begin to embrace yourself, your purpose begins to clearly manifest itself and you realize why you were created the way you are. You begin to understand that the world needs you exactly how you are.

I would be foolish to act as if my spirituality had no direct effect on the brave acceptance of myself. Although I know everyone's religious beliefs and preferences may vary, I can only give an account of what worked and helped me. Along with time and growth, there were three specific scriptures that caused my life to drastically change and reach the place of peace where I am today: 1 Corinthians 13:4-8, Jeremiah 29:11 and Galatians 6:9.

Love! There, I said it; the one word that I believe has the capability to rule and overpower everything. I am an advocate for love. Self-love and acceptance are just a small portion of the power behind love. My all-time favorite passage is found in 1 Corinthians and is my life guide to how I operate. I could literally go on for hours about this passage because it is so essential and beautiful. If I am honest, this passage is my solution to almost everything; *love, love, love*. Therefore, many people question what love is: this passage describes it so perfectly. 1 Corinthians 13:4-8 states: "Love is patient, love is kind, it does not envy, it does not boast, it is not proud. It does not dishonor others, it is not self-seeking, it is not easily angered, it keeps no record of wrongs. Love does not delight in evil but rejoices with the truth. It always protects, always trusts, always hopes, always preserves. Love never fails." This scripture shows us the foundation of life. Imagine love in this context being utilized by the actions of people every day. I remember constantly saying people have a love problem, and that love is the solution to most of our unequal endeavors. I believe all the answers to our dilemmas today have easy answers, but we find difficulty in acting out those answers. I can easily sit here and state that love is the answer, but love will not necessarily manifest itself just because we are suddenly aware of the solution. My job as a fellow follower of Christ is not to make you love, but to present you with the knowledge of knowing this is the answer. Before one can truly learn to love others, one must first learn to love God and one's self. As you can see, I struggled with this because there was a point in my life where I had only a small amount of love for myself; I despised most things about me. This scripture helped me to realize exactly what love is and taught me how to apply it in my own life. Once I was able to love myself, I was able to allow my love for others and life to pour outwardly. Love is so much more powerful than we give it credit for. We throw the word out so loosely, but are we truly loving according to what the word describes love to be. We know when we are walking and living in love because it never fails; so if it fails, was it ever love? I consider my heart to be both my greatest strength and my greatest weakness. Without perfection, I know that my intentions are pure when operating in love, so I can rest knowing I try to do right. Consequently, doing so also creates a state of vulnerability that can easily be manipulated and misused. Thankfully, it is undoubtedly my greatest asset because I have learned to love genuinely: this is my prayer for each of us.

When I was younger, Jeremiah 29:11 was by far was my favorite scripture because it reminded me of purpose. I struggled with an internal identity problem. I did not feel special and lacked purpose, nor did I feel like I belonged or even deserved much of anything at one point. Thankfully, this scripture states: "For I know the plans I have for you declares the Lord, plans to prosper you and not to harm you, plans to give you hope and a future." It reminded me that God has a plan for me, for Kristal; it meant I was not overlooked or forgotten. I can always remember that I was never a mistake. God has a plan for me, to give me hope, and a future regardless of what negative thoughts try to convince me or where I find myself. I constantly read this scripture and prayed to understand it in its totality anytime I felt worthless. I am at an age now where I can be vocal and transparent about the demons I have faced. My newfound confidence in myself causes me to look back and ask, "how dare I think so low of myself?" I get upset at the wasted tears and years of utter frustration that was unnecessary at the time. Purpose is predestined and God never changed his mind; feeling invaluable or doubtful does not affect what God previously promised you. I am a firm believer in what God has for me is for me. Live life in confidence knowing that nothing or anyone can take that from you.

An optimistic scripture that allows me to be who I am is none

other than Galatians 6:9. It states:
"Let us not become weary in doing
good, for at the proper time we will
reap a harvest if we do not give up."
Often times, I felt like doing good
was pointless and that I would
always get the short end of the stick.
I can remember asking God why I
had to be bothered with a conscience
and convictions eating at my spirit
with certain thoughts that came to
mind. I felt like being a "good"
person was getting me nowhere.
People would take advantage of you,
treat you in ways you would never
treat them, and I was unable to
understand why "good" people
finished last. This scripture aids in
remembering that at the right time,
we will reap our harvest. I actually
have come to terms with and
accepted that it may not even be in
this lifetime. However, I believe
God's word so I know it will pay off
one day just like He said it would.
One of the major keys to remember
in this Christian walk is that there will

be darkness. We were born into inequity, but there is hope in believing that we are the light. Be the light where there is darkness and never let the darkness consume your light. Good people do not finish last. One of the most humbling lessons I learned as a young adult is that the world will not treat you any better just because you are a good person; conversely, a good person does not stop being a good person because of a few bad people. Believe it or not, your light is needed, even by those who may seem to push it away.

Life is the most unpredictable adventure we will all experience. The ability to be in control of everything was taken away from us the second we were born. No two people were dealt the same cards; even identical twins have different thought processes and personalities that takes them on different paths of life. We all have the ability to determine how we decide to play our cards. Smaller hands are not destined to lose; determination wins. Our biggest setback is our inner selves and this turns out to be our enemy. We allow ourselves to overthink and question our existence at times because of the circumstances surrounding us. Those thoughts of being an outcast make us feel like we do not fit in when we were created to stand out. Our comparisons to other people and the temptations around us can cause us to not be grateful for the assets we do have. Human people have human feelings. We hurt, overcompensate, infuriate, fight, cry, laugh, smile, love, and even hate. In those moments when we are down and at our lowest, it is imperative that we do not stay there. Changing your thinking will drastically change your life. If you have dealt with similar feelings of isolation, loneliness, outcast, and rejection like me, know that perspective is your way out. If you consistently feel like you have never ideally fit anywhere, maybe it is time for you to create your own place of belonging. Moreover, maybe you are wanting to fit into places and with people who are not destined to go where you are called to go. Your isolation could be for your protection. When your focus shifts from wondering why you have what you have to what to do with what you have is when vision and purpose start to manifest. Whether you constantly feel like the third wheel or on the outside looking in, if you truly reflect on your life, you realize you have everything you need to accomplish every dream and desire of your heart--you always have.

# About the Author

Kristal Ben was born and raised in Ville Platte, LA. She is the youngest daughter of Tillman and Jeanita Ben. She is a proud graduate of Grambling State University. Kristal has always been passionate about writing and using it as a tool to help impact and inflict change in others. Her prayer is that this is only the beginning of a new journey and that someone is inspired through her story.

www.ingramcontent.com/pod-product-compliance
Lightning Source LLC
Chambersburg PA
CBHW052143220626
47052CB00005B/1169